What A SISTER Won't Do

CHARLES L. WALTON

What a Sister Won't Do

Published and designed by Ministry Event Marketing.

Printed in the United States of America

ISBN: 979-8-9986757-8-2   Paperback

TABLE OF CONTENTS

CHAPTER ONE

"Tequila Caprice Stone! Getcho' ass up, right now!" `Tequila, at once, did what her mother demanded. In a flash, she sat upright in her bed, and her mother was standing at the foot of it. "Turn on the damn lights!" Tequila did it again, as Mother ordered, and flicked the switch on her wall.

The issue was that DN was there, sleeping over. It surely wasn't his first time sleeping over, but the fact that he did, at all, was supposed to remain unbeknownst to Ms. Long, but the jig was now up. DN was Tequila's newborn's father. He was just 20 years old, and Tequila was only 19. The two had just given birth to a baby boy three months before.

"Hello, Ms. Long," he sleepily came.

"Shut up, DN!" Ms. Long felt absolutely no compunction about discovering them in her home. She was only peeking into her daughter's room. checking on her grandson late that night, and caught them.

"Momma, I can explain."

"I don't want to hear shit you've got to say! And DN, you should be downright ashamed of yourself! I feel sorry for my grandson. His mother's a slut, and his father ain't no damn man!" Tequila and DN said nothing back. They had nothing of any value to say back.

CHAPTER TWO

Eventually, Ms. Long sat at the kitchen table with Tequila and DN and listened to them discuss the fact that DN had been kicked onto the streets by his own mother and stepfather. Because of that, they said he had been occasionally sleeping over. They claimed he had nowhere else to go.

By the end of their talk, Ms. Long pitied her grandson's father a bit and said he was allowed to stay. That was after, of course, he'd promised to get a job and help out with the bills and the groceries. He presently wasn't employed. He was simply a young dude in the neighborhood who didn't do much or have much. He promised to change all of that. That was three months ago.

CHAPTER THREE

One afternoon, DN was at the house, playing video games on the floor, as Tequila and the baby boy were sleeping in the bed, when a knock sounded at the door. He asked, Who is it?" Three times and got no response. After the third time, he got up from the video game he was playing and again yelled, "Who is it!" and again got no verbal response. The thing of it was that whoever it was never answered but kept periodically knocking.

DN walked to and just opened the door. As soon as he did, he was jacked up and roughed up, and forced back into the house by two muscular dudes. One punched him in the stomach. One

5

punched him in the face. Then out came the rope and tape.

CHAPTER FOUR

Behind them, in walked another clearly muscular dude; even through his nice suit pants and jacket, one could see the bulges. The sharp-dressed, clean, bald, Black man looked to be in his mid-thirties. He was standing back while the first two continued very roughly, roughing up a totally clueless DN. He had no idea who, in the hell, they were, or what in the hell their issue was.

For a moment, they paused, and the bald guy approached and calmly, with a straight face, said, "DN, you owe me... You're going to pay me, too." The goons were holding DN to standing up and still. The goon, on his right, punched him in the face; the other landed a real hard body shot.

The bald man calmly strolled around, admiring the house. Then he called out, "Tie his hands up." The two goons promptly took DN down, then one pulled some twine out of his pocket and tied his hands up.

"Now, who's in the room?" The bald man came close.

Scared shitless, DN stuttered, "P-P-Please don't go in there. It's—it's—it's just my baby momma and my son. They're sleeping. Please don't go in there." He still didn't know what the hell was going on.

"Oh, but we must." The man then instructed the goons, "Tape his mouth." One of them pulled out a roll of duct tape and covered DN's mouth.

Then he tore off the rest of the roll.

The four of them then opened the door and went into the bedroom, where Tequila was lying, sweetly embracing the baby as they lay. There was one chair in the room in which the goons sat DN in. The bald man just coolly stood at the door and watched. Tequila and the baby did not stir. The bald man then nodded his head at the goons and said, "Let's wake her ass up. The one on his left side then snatched DN's fake earring off his ear. DN's mouth was taped shut, but he still yelled loud enough to wake Tequila.

She shot up to a sitting position to see three strange, muscular men in her room with DN tied, taped, and swollen-eyed, with blood dripping from his ear. She was blown away. At first, she didn't know what to say or do. She then yelled, "Who in the hell are you motherfuckers? Get out of my

damn room!" The child then woke up crying.

CHAPTER FIVE

"Ma'am, I am Jerrel Tate. Maybe you've heard of me?" In fact, she had. Jerrel Tate was a notorious mob figure in the city of Tampa. All the girls wanted to be with him, and all the guys wanted to be like him. The closest that most came, though, was just hearing about him or seeing him on the news. To some, he was a myth, and to some, he was the damn truth.

CHAPTER SIX

"Sir, I don't give a damn who you are. Get outta my damn room!" With that, the baby started bawling. At first, Jerrel Tate was just coolly standing in the doorway. When the extra loud crying started, he walked over to Tequila, extended his arms and hands, and said, "Gimme." After he stood there for a moment, she gave him the baby. There was a half-drunk baby bottle on the dresser that Jerrel Tate scooped up and began feeding the baby boy with.

He was gently cradling and feeding the child when he started talking again. "Rule number one is shut the fuck up when I'm talking, and that goes for everyone."

Highly nervous and agitated, Tequila came out with, "Well, hurry up and say whatcha got to say and give me back my baby." Jerrel Tate stopped talking and looked over at the goons and nodded his head. One goon then punched DN hard in the ribs. "Now, ma'am, can I please have your undivided attention?"

"Yeah, but gimme back my baby." - Tequila

Jerrel Tate looked over at his goons again and nodded. This time, the other one punched DN hard in the face.

"Now, ma'am, if you would be so kind as to let me finish, I will be out of you people's house and hair in no time." He then spoke of Alonzo (who is no longer with us). He commented on how he had killed a man and stole a few barrels of weed. He said that the guy he killed belonged to a rival Cuban gang. He said that his own deceased father and the leader of that Cuban gang had a long-standing beef. He said that since his father's passing, things had been cooling down and getting a whole lot better for everyone, then Alonzo did what he did and messed everything up.

CHAPTER SEVEN

He continued calmly speaking of his awareness of DN's deal with Alonzo and DN's subsequent deal with the friend, who was hard to track down these days. He said that he knew about the thousand dollars and all.

He then got up, in DN's face, "Look here, boy, you owe me those six thousand dollars. I know you don't have it right now, but please know I'll be back every week for my money, ya understand?"

"Yes, sir," he screamed and audibly mumbled through the tape. Jerrel Tate looked up at his goons, smiled, and nodded his head. One punched

DN hard in the side. "Now I could have let that one slide, but what I'm trying to show you is that I don't let anything slide, ever, especially when it's about my money."

"Now, DN, every time I come and you ain't got my money, it's going to go up another grand, and I'm gon' leave you with a little reminder to go and get my money, ya understand?" This time, DN didn't say anything but shook his head up and down. Jerrel Tate and his goons chuckled. "There ya go. That's a lot better, ain't it?"

Again, DN nodded his head. "Now, I promise you, I'll be back next week." Jerrel Tate then kindly walked back over and handed Tequila her baby, saying, "You probably want to burp him. Then, he and the goons walked out of the whole house. As soon as the front door was heard closing, Tequila hopped up and scurried over to the window and looked to see what kind of car they were in, but they were already gone.

Tequila then came back into the room, picked up the baby, sat on the edge of the bed, and crossly looked at DN, who didn't look so good right then. His eye was severely swollen, his wrists were tied, his mouth was taped over, and his ear was still bleeding. She just looked at him.

.

CHAPTER EIGHT

Tequila then rose and snatched the tape off of DN's mouth."

"Oh, thank you," he breathed out. "Now I gotta get this…"

Tequila sharply interrupted him. "So, you had a thousand dollars?" She said that with much attitude.

DN looked back at her with a wide-eyed, disbelieving gaze. He raised his arms a bit and said, "What about my ear?"

"Fuck yo ear. You got another one. "What about the thousand dollars, DN?"

"Please, baby," he pleaded. Tequila didn't move.

She rolled her neck and peered at him closely.

"I'm listening," Tequila said

At first, DN was blowed, he huffed big time, then he came with, "Where do you think the LeBrons' and the two video game consoles with updated remote controls and headphones came from? And remember... I did buy the baby some Pampers... Remember?"

Tequila smacked her disappointed lips in disbelief. "So, you had a thousand dollars and bought some sneakers and some video games and lied to me and said you were holdin'em, for your cousin?"

"Nah, I bought the baby some Pampers, too.

And my friend was supposed to pay me five thousand mo'."

"Are you serious, dude?"

She then laid the baby down and left the room. She returned shortly with a pair of scissors and cut loose his bound-together wrists.

CHAPTER NINE

"So, you had a thousand damn dollars?" moped Tequila as she dropped her butt down on the bed. He was in the bathroom, seeing about his still-bleeding ear. Tequila, noticeably, wasn't speaking to him. In the times he'd ask for her assistance, she'd ignore him and continue doing what she was doing at that time.

Hours later, during the time when DN went on his now daily search for his friend, who owed him five thousand dollars. Tequila's older sister Tisa came by the house. She used her door key to enter, and as soon as she did, she came right into Tequila's bedroom. "Where is my lil' man?" She went straight to and scooped up Tequila's son, peppering him with kisses. "Mr. Dynamite" was what she'd dubbed him. "How's my little Mr. Dynamite?" She then loudly blew a kiss on his belly. He laughed.

Tisa thought the world of her nephew. She immensely loved her sister, but she didn't think very highly of DN. She referred to him as "the little boy with nothing to offer" behind his back and in front of him. Tisa would make funny and offensive remarks at his expense. She'd make light of his very being, even making jokes about why his own parents had ousted him. When Tequila told about the visit paid to their mom's home by Jerel Tate and his goons, Tisa angrily replied, "See, T... That's why you need to stop fucking with that... that super trifling motherfucker."

"He said he had another friend who knew how to get in touch with the friend who owed him five thousand dollars."

"And you believed him? Chile… Better you than me. Ain't no way I could have a sorry, video game-playing 'nigga like that around me. I'm finna go home, girl. C'mere, Mr. Dynamite." She scooped up and playfully kissed her nephew, and then she left.

CHAPTER TEN

There was a difference between Tequila and Tisa, and the difference showed itself in the way they lived. While Tequila was still at home, living with their mom. Tisa was a real "go-getter girl" who moved out and had been living on her own since the age of 20. She was now 26 and in a committed relationship.

Her love was a 29-year-old, biracial guy with aspirations of becoming a political figure. His mother was white, and his dad was a Black man. He was currently setting out to become Tampa's next mayor. That night, while lying in bed, Tisa shared with him the same news Tequila had relayed to her, and immediately, he got very upset. "Please don't get involved at all with that. Just the name Jerrel Tate could ruin any chances of becoming mayor!"

"I know, baby, but I don't like the fact that he's coming to my mom's house."

"Me either; that's why we have to keep any dealings involving him out of public knowledge." He pushed Tisa to agree before they went to sleep.

CHAPTER ELEVEN

"Girl, those are some badass shoes," remarked a valued customer at the bank Tisa was employed at.

"Thank ya, thank ya," coolly replied Tisa to the lady she was sitting at her desk with. "They sure cost enough."

"Girl, you be doing ya thang."

"I can't keep up with you, though. Miss Gucci Suit." The two Black women chuckled a bit, then got down to the business at hand. It was a simple money transfer. The amount was astounding, as usual, with the woman, as usual. "If you don't mind me asking, what is it that you do?" The truth was that the woman was a personal customer of hers, and her name was Bliss Tate. Tisa was very careful but had decided to launch a small-scale investigation. For all she knew, she was doing business with and was very friendly with the wife of the gangster Jerrel Tate.

"It's not me; it's my husband's money. Don't even get me started on that man. I don't even know for sure what he does. He always says he's in the contractual business, whatever that means."

"I just asked because it seems like you guys are always doing so well."

"Chile, I couldn't tell ya what exactly he does." The women laughed and then said their "goodbyes."

CHAPTER TWELVE

"So DN, what the hell are you doin' today?"

"I've gotta go pawn this stuff."

"Humph," Tequila responded. It had been a day short of a week since Jerrel Tate's last visit, and thus far, DN hadn't amassed anything. He also had not seen or heard from his friend. He had spoken with his other friend, who said that he had not seen the first friend in weeks.

CHAPTER THIRTEEN

The next day, the much-anticipated knock came on the door, scaring DN to the point of almost urinating on himself. Like normal, he asked, "Who is it?" When it sounded, it got no response. When the same thing happened a second time, with the periodical knocking, he was sure it was them.

When DN rose and opened the door again, he was roughly greeted by the same two goons from the first time. Immediately, he was jacked up and forced back into the house. "Wait, wait, wait, wait! I have some money!" At once, the goons put him back down on his feet. Then in strolled Jerrel Tate, who softly shut the door behind him. Today, his suit was sharp and all gray, on top of sharp gray dress shoes.

DN then dug into his pocket and produced the five hundred and twelve dollars he'd gotten the day before at the pawn shop. That was what he'd gotten back for the video game consoles, their headphones, mouthpieces, and all their other accessories. Also, he'd pawned his shoes.

Jerrel Tate walked up to him, looked at the money, and said, "You keep that. I'm here for my money, and that ain't it. We now are at seven thousand dollars." He then eyed the goons and said, "Make him understand." The goons then proceeded to beat him up a bit. The first one decked him in the face. The second one nailed him in the ribs. They did it a second time, with the two goons alternating their punch spots. They did it another time after that, too. When they stopped, DN dropped to the floor. "My girl, in there?" Jerrel Tate looked down and asked DN.

"No," he whimpered.

Jerrel Tate opened the door and went in anyway. Tequila was standing there, holding her child. "Hi, Mr. Tate."

"Mr. Tate was my father. To you, I'm just Jerrel, sweety, he smiled. "How's the baby?" he kindly asked.

"Oh, he's good." Tequila then spun, so he could get a better view of the child.

CHAPTER FOURTEEN

"He came again?" said surprised Tisa when Tequila told her.

"Yup."

"And all they did was beat up DN and leave though, right?"

"Yup."

"He's okay though, right?

"Yeah, he alright, or will be alright."

"Where is the boy now?"

"He went to see some friend of his." Tequila and Tisa aimlessly chatted a bit more before Tisa left.

CHAPTER FIFTEEN

"So you're saying that all we have to do is take that car to the "chop shop," and yo people gon' give us 25 hunnet' fo' it and you gon' gimme 15?" "Yeah, man. That's it. It's already set up and erethang'." DN had a friend, who's uncle ran a 'chop shop' and DN had previously told him of his money woes, so the friend, being a friend, was trying to slide DN in on a quick way to put a few dollars in his pocket. DN said he was down with it.

The deal was specific, for a rare foreign 'sup'd up' Porsche, with a very rare 'sup'd up' engine. Without keys to it, they were in line to score only

500 dollars, but with keys, the uncle was going to bless them with $2500. In light of all that, DN and his friend were making plans to 'carjack' the driver and take his keys.

CHAPTER SIXTEEN

"Dear, it is truly imperative that you stay away and out of that whole mess!" These were the words of Tisa's lover when she told him about Jerrel Tate's most recent visit to her mom's house.

"I agree, but this dude is coming to my mother's house, and I really want that to stop, like yesterday!"

"I don't like it either, but the upcoming race for this city's next mayor is only six months away, and the last thing we need is to be involved in anything involving him! We have to stay as far away from

Jerrel Tate as possible! I'm getting ready to start making signs, so I've got to think about my image! I really want this to work, for us!"

"I mean, you're right and all; it's just that it's a bit too close for comfort."

"I can relate to that, but we don't need that swirling anywhere around us right now." "I really do agree, baby, but…"

"Dear, we really really don't need this right now. It's hard enough trying to get people to vote for a zebra, and this Jerrel Tate shit will murder my political career.

CHAPTER SEVENTEEN

"No DN. Get away from me." DN was going in for a little sex with his son's mother. She was holding him at bay, though. At the same time, she was sexually active with one of her other men. The other guy had a car and an apartment. He was a blossoming, young drug dealer.

"Besides DN, you need to be concerned with getting your coins together before Jerrel Tate comes back."

"Yeah, yeah…"

"Alright now, you know, when that man comes, you get scared."

"So?" He didn't even deny it. "You need to mind yo business, girl. Besides, ain't you supposed to be my girl?"

"Shut yo' lil' scary butt up." DN did just that and left.

He walked to his friend's house, who happened to be on the porch. When he walked up, his friend dapped him and asked, "Nigga you ready?"

"Ready for what?" DN asked back.

"To go get this money." This was the same friend, with the uncle, with the 'chop shop.'

"Yeah. I mean, I thought we were supposed to do that tomorrow."

"Yeah, but some shit came up. You ain't the only one that needs money. Plus, I got the perfect plan... We just gon' wait, at the gas station for'em. He went and grabbed his, 22 caliber handgunand handed it to DN. DN took the gun and then looked strangely at his friend. DN took it but gave him a strange look. "I got one too, fool. Chill out. Just c'mon." The friend turned and stepped. DN followed.

The two strolled half a mile to the corner store with plans of waiting there for the guy to come and get some gas. It wasn't long before just that happened.

CHAPTER EIGHTEEN

When the car pulled into being, at the gas pump. DN was to pull the pistol on the guy and demand the keys when he got out. His friend was to hold down the other side of the car in case there were any heroes who wanted to spring into action. Nothing that they had planned for went down the way they'd planned.

For starters, the guy, who was usually driving the car, wasn't even in the car. A female over sixty climbed out of the driver's seat. DN looked over at his friend, who was also shocked but signaled DN to wait until she came out of the store and then go along with their plan.

When the woman exited the store and was walking back to the car, DN stepped along beside her. He stepped beside her and said, "Hey lady, just gimme the car keys." He had his gun out, by his side. She looked down and saw the gun and was immediately startled. "What the hell do you want, son?"

"Just gimme the keys, ma'am."

"But my momma is in the car," she loudly returned. As she was saying that, DN's friend had snatched open the passenger door and saw the 80-year-old lady, complete with walker and everything.

Thinking that they were already in too deep to turn around, DN forcefully said, "Just gimme the damn keys, lady!"

She gave him her entire purse, saying, "I'm sure they're in there." Also, at that time, DN's friend was assisting the other older lady out of the car. Ultimately, the two friends got in and drove off.

CHAPTER NINETEEN

That night DN bragged to Tequila that he had went and hit a lick. She, however, was not impressed and still didn't give him any. He still slept on the floor in her room. She let him use a pillow off her bed and gave him a sheet. He had no choice but to be satisfied with that.

As of now, DN had around two thousand dollars. He called his friend that night, saying that they needed to do that a few more times. The friend just said, "Okay," then hung up.

DN went to the local daily labor office twice more but saw that as futile. He would only make 40 bucks a day there. He'd washed two cars there, at the house, at ten dollars, a pop, before Tequila scolded him about using her mother's water like that. He was forced to forfeit that venture.

CHAPTER TWENTY

Another week rolled around, and Jerrel Tate and his goons were at the door again. This time, DN was standing outside, waiting for them. The two goons, in Dickie suits, walked up on him first, with the nicely dressed Jerrel Tate right behind them. This time, his suit and shoes were blue.

The three muscular men strolled up to him, with sour looks on their faces, and Jerrel Tate came out with, "Don't you think it would be more appropriate if we took this inside, DN? Being outside ain't gon' save you." DN was already nervous.

"But wait, I got two thousand dollars for ya." Flatly, Jerrel Tate came back, but you owe me seven." DN had no choice, but to turn and step back in. The three men followed him.

As soon as they got inside, the goons jacked DN up, giving him a punch apiece. Jerrel Tate then walked up to him. "We ain't gon' keep waisting our time beating you up. This time we goin' with knives. One of the goons sprang out, with a switchblade and popped it. DN was horrified. He tried to make a dash, to the bedroom but didn't make it past the muscular goons.

They took him to the floor, and the one with the knife coarsely shaved off one of DN's eyebrows. Jerrel Tate stood back and laughed. Then he opened the bedroom door, where Tequila was standing, holding the baby boy. Jerrel Tate told her to come and look at DN. She did and laughed heartily at her son's father, who was still lying on his back on the ground.

DN, by nature, had especially thick eyebrows. It was a trait passed throughout his family.

CHAPTER TWENTY-ONE

"This shit has got to stop!" Tisa was full of anger as she relayed what Tequila had told her about Jerrel Tate and his goons coming by their mom's house again. She was furious.

"You said all they did was shave off the boy's eyebrow."

"Yeah, it's funny, and he looks ridiculous, lemme tell ya, but can't we get tem, for breaking and entering?"

"Nah, because they were invited in."

"There has got to be something…"

"Nope, dear, they didn't break any laws."

"This shit has got to stop." "There is nothing we can do, dear.

Your mom still doesn't know anything, about it?"

"No. She still don't know nothin'. I'm scared, for her."

"Why, dear?"

"Because they're comin' to her house."

"Now, now… dear. We don't have anything to do with it, though? Because that would be downright murder for my run for office."

CHAPTER TWENTY-TWO

"Look DN…" Ms. Long had sat DN down and was talking to him. "Now I've let you come and stay in my house for a few months now, and you still haven't come forth with anything. Son, I'll give you another week, and then, I'm afraid, you have to go. I believe I've been more than fair with allowing you to stay here. And what happened to your eyebrow?"

DN had nothing he could say back, except hanging his head and coming back, "Yes, ma'am." He never went into the whole 'eyebrow' thing. Tequila was not there at the time. She'd taken the baby to the doctor earlier and, unbeknownst to DN, got picked

up by her other guy. That was a lot earlier that day.

CHAPTER TWENTY-THREE

Since the night of his talk, with Ms. Long, DN had been going daily to the day labor office. Also, he'd been hounding his friend about them stealing another car, but the friend had nothing for them. On the day Jerrel Tate was due to come by, though, he stayed home, electing to go ahead and face the music rather than have the goons seek him out. He estimated that that would be worse. That day, though, Jerrel Tate and only one goon showed up, like an hour later than normal.

DN manned up and went and opened on the door's first knock. He anticipated being immediately jacked up. He'd been doing push-ups and all, in anticipation. However, his anticipation was all wrong.

When he cracked the door open and peeked out, the well-dressed Jerrel Tate and the one goon were just standing there looking back at him. With no aggression, they pushed the door and went inside.

As soon as they were in, DN went into stuttering and apologizing. On a closer look, one could see the somberness the two men had within them. They came in and grabbed chairs, for them to sit in. They sat, and Jerrel Tate told him that the other goon was murdered by the Cubans the night before. He said that that guy was a real friend of his. He said that he really wasn't up for the usual violence right then. He admitted, "I don't even know why I came here." He said that while manfully wiping his eyes. He and the one goon then rose and were leaving, when the cat named

Son ran out. Jerrel Tate went down and scooped up the cat and continued stepping, only turning back to face DN and tell him, "I'll just be keeping this until you come up with my money. We are now at eight thousand. All DN could do was stand there and watch. He couldn't help but speak out, "Hey man, you can't do that." "Watch me. If you want'em back, come up with my damn money."

CHAPTER TWENTY-FOUR

"Girl, you will never believe what my husband has done!" Tisa was sitting again, with Mrs. Tate, at her bank desk. With special interest, she was listening attentively to her. "He brought home a damn cat! A big, grown-ass cat! The kids love it, but all I can think is that that is someone's cat. He won't tell me where he got the damn cat from. He says a friend gave it to him to hold for a while while he's outta town. I don't believe him, though. All I know is the kids ain't gon' wanna hear that shit, about givin' him back, when the friend comes home."

The night before, Tequila had already told Tisa about Jerrel Tate's last visit and his taking of Son.

Ms. Long was distraught and took off work that next day, just in case Son wandered back. Tequila hadn't told her the truth about Son's disappearance and whereabouts.

The story Tequila went with and was sticking with, to their mother, was that she'd left the front door open while cleaning the house, and it was then that the cat must have escaped, undetected. With few questions, her mother bought it. Tisa on the other hand, was livid.

Tisa and her man got into a huge, huge argument after she told him about the whole 'Jerrel Tate- cat' thing. His stance was that they should not get involved at all with it. Her stance was, "Fuck you and the damn mayor shit! I'm gonna help my momma get her cat back!" Well into the night they went back and forth, with neither side giving any ground. That night, Tisa ended up leaving and getting a hotel room.

CHAPTER TWENTY-FIVE

The thing was that when Tisa spoke last, with Mrs. Tate, she paid special attention to Jerrel Tate picking the kids up from school most days. She also learned that he took on the responsibility of getting their daughter to and from her ballet practices and recitals. She said she did the same for their son and football. From this, Tisa had the idea of tracking him down and seducing him to get her mom's cat back.

After two days of noticing that Jerrel Tate would go to the same nearby coffee shop after dropping his daughter, at practice, she went in and sat at the open table next to his. She was careful to seem, as casual as possible, though she made sure she looked damn good and smelled even better. By happenstance, she struck up an aimless conversation with him.

They talked, smiled, and laughed for quite a bit. They were genuinely enjoying each other's company. Her story was that her name was Lisa and she was briefly in town for a seminar for her job. She was an accountant for an unheard-of tech company. He said he was in the consultation field. Though Tisa knew why she was really there, she couldn't get over how good-looking, sharply dressed, and muscular and how nice Jerrel Tate was.

When Jerrel Tate looked at his watch, he saw that his daughter's class had been over half an hour ago. Before saying their goodbyes, they agreed to meet again the next day, at that same place, at the same time.

CHAPTER TWENTY-SIX

That very next day, at that very same time, Jerrel Tate stepped in that very same coffee shop and sat, at the table, across from Tisa (Lisa). She had gotten there, like, 10 minutes before him. They were happy to see each other again. They hugged. He was muscular, sharply dressed, and good-looking, again, and she was 'wine fine,' again, in a low-cut blouse and a nice dress with a high slit on the side, showing off her long hairless legs.

The two sat and chatted, at length, again. An hour or so into their conversing, Jerrel Tate felt that it was only right for him to mention that he was a married man. He said that he had to tell her that because he was obviously attracted to her. He went on to explain that he couldn't see how any man wouldn't be. At first, she simply blushed and said, "Thank you," to each compliment he gave her. She then divulged her sexual attraction to him. Again they sat and did a lot of smiling, as they extensively chatted about this, that, and the other.

Before they gathered themselves to leave, they agreed that a motel room for them was in order. It just so happened that his daughter did not have practice that next night. Lisa admitted to having the 'hots' for him right then. Jerrel Tate said that normally he would never cheat on his wife. Lisa said that she hated that they met under these conditions. She also salaciously said that she just had to fuck him, one time, though. They agreed, to rendezvous at the Double Tree hotel that next evening.

Lisa was forward, with telling him that she would get there before him and would already be in the room, dressed or undressed and ready, awaiting his arrival. Jerrel Tate agreed to it and said he couldn't wait!. Lisa kissed his cheek when they embraced before parting. They exchanged phone numbers.

CHAPTER TWENTY-SEVEN

The next day, at 5:46 am, Jerrel Tate called Lisa. She said she was already in the room that she gave him the number to. The room was an expensive one, all the way, on the top floor. Jerrel Tate caught the elevator, up to it. When he knocked on the room door, Lisa swung it open and looked so very appealing and even delicious to him. He looked the same way to her.

When he came in, the two embraced and kissed a bit. It was clear that both of them had thrown caution to the wind for this event. Jerrel Tate wore a dark purple suit, with a light purple shirt and some unbelievably fly purple shoes. On their initial hug and kiss, Lisa was deeply turned on by whatever cologne he had on.

She invited him to have a seat in one of the two chairs at the table, where she already had drinks poured for him and for herself. They sat and began drinking.

CHAPTER TWENTY-EIGHT

After laughing and downing their first drink, Lisa poured them another. Lisa then helped Jerrel Tate out of his jacket and urged him to relax while she slipped into the bathroom to put on something more suitable for what they'd planned to do.

Made in the USA
Columbia, SC
23 August 2025